Cloudy

WITH A CHANCE OF RAIN

SUNNYVILLE SERIES BOOK 1

WRITTEN BY
JOSEPH WARTTS

ILLUSTRATED BY
CHRISTOPHER WARTTS

Cloudy With A Chance Of Rain

Inquiries should be addressed to:

JWartts Publishing, LLC
5 Bertha Place Ct.
Florissant, MO 63034

First Edition

2 3 4 5 6 7 8 9 10

Library of Congress Cataloging-in-Publication
Data is available.
ISBN 10:   1717400329
ISBN 13:   978-1717400321

Illustrations by Christopher Wartts
Edited by Gleevia Wartts
Additional Edits by Dr. Stanley Berry

Thanks

All glory, honor and thanks to our Lord and Savior Jesus Christ for all that has been given to me and particularly in this instance, the creative inspiration and courage needed to attempt this work.

My Sincere Thanks To:

My wife, Alicia, for her love and enthusiastic support and encouragement.

My daughters, Jordyn and Lauren, whose utterance of the same observation, "Dad, it looks like the clouds are crying," (separately, and amazingly, 15 years apart) inspired this journey.

Gleevia Wartts and Christopher Wartts for their enduring spirit through all of the phone calls, emails, and for their hard work and dedication to this book.

Naima Wartts, Jean Carr, Stephanie Wilson, Charles Wartts, Bertha Franks, Cheryl Morris-Wartts, Jaylen Wilson, De Alma Foree, Kim and Avery Landsman, Dr. Stanley Berry and his granddaughter Ava, for taking the time to read the book and for their encouragement and critical feedback.

This book is dedicated to my parents Lillie and Charlie Wartts, whose example of, hard work, faith in the face of hardship; and their unspoken need to push forward, despite life's challenges, is the basis for who I am.

CONTENTS

WEATHERMAN BLUES

"It's going to be another *bea-uuu-tiful* day in Sunnyville, folks!" exclaimed weatherman, Robert Michael Fox, better known as Big Bob. "It will be sunny with a high of 75 and for tonight, clear with a low of 68. So get out those grills! It's time for some good ole bar-be-que!" he added brightly, winking at the camera.

"Cut! And we're clear," Steve Robinson, News Director and Station Manager of Sunnyville TV Station KJSV, called out to Big Bob and the studio crew. "Great job, Big Bob! That's another *outstanding* forecast!" Steve gushed.

"Thanks, Steve," Big Bob said with a small sigh, leaving his cheery on camera personality behind. "I'll see you all tomorrow," he said, hanging his head slightly as he walked slowly back to his office.

"What's the matter with Big Bob?" Ollie, the news anchor, asked Steve. "He seems so sad lately."

"I don't know," answered Steve. "He always gives such great weather reports. By gosh, he's the most popular guy in town! What would *he* have to be sad about?" Steve asked, genuinely puzzled.

Bob, the country's youngest weatherman, and Ollie, its youngest news anchor, had both graduated and received their respective degrees in Meteorology and Journalism, at age fourteen. Steve, the station manager, was so impressed when he saw their audition tapes that he offered them both jobs immediately after they graduated. The station had garnered nationwide attention as a result.

In fact, Station KJSV's nightly newscast had the highest rating in the country, leading the nearest competitor by double digits. Certainly, as far as Steve was concerned, Bob had little reason to be sad.

FAST FRIENDS

Bob was slender, with medium brown skin and wore his hair cut into a short Afro. Growing up, he was noticeably shorter than most boys his age, but, thanks to a recent growth spurt, he was now 6-foot-4—a change dramatic enough to earn him the nickname, "Big Bob."

His clothes were always neat: a precisely pressed shirt, dress pants, and suspenders instead of a belt. He wore glasses and carried a briefcase (even back in grade school!) to keep his books and papers organized.

Ollie Lopez was petite with caramel-colored skin and long brown hair which was always pulled straight back into a ponytail. Back when she was a student, she wore thick bifocals and baggy clothes, all of which served to mask how pretty she was. She had come into her own since then, however, and made quite an attractive impression behind the news desk during her broadcast. Like Bob, Ollie believed in carrying a briefcase.

From the first day of school when they met in Mrs. Henderson's kindergarten class, Bob and Ollie had been best friends. Partly because of the way they looked back then, and partly because they were both so smart, they endured teasing and online bullying throughout grade and high school. "Nerd twins" and "eggheads" were just two of the unkind nicknames some of the other kids called them.

Over time, however, their shared trials, together with their triumphs, only brought them closer.

A DIFFERENT SORT OF TOWN

As to why Big Bob seemed so sad, well—it had a *lot* to do with his hometown of Sunnyville.

You see, Sunnyville was different from other towns. It had the very same weather each day—of each week—of each year. Nothing ever changed. It was always sunny on Saturdays, Sundays, and Mondays. Every Tuesday and Wednesday, it was partly cloudy, with some sunshine. You could count on Thursdays to be dreary and overcast. And, lastly, no one ever had to wonder what to expect on Fridays because it rained all day.

In this strange and special town, it never got hotter than 75 degrees during the day or colder than 68 degrees at night. As far back as anyone could remember, Sunnyville's weather had been consistent this way, and the townspeople were happy about it because they always knew what to expect and how to dress for the coming day. Things had gone on like this for so long, in fact, that no one even thought to question how it all came to be.

THE SUNNYVILLE WEATHER AGREEMENT

What the people of Sunnyville didn't know, was that the town's safe and comfortable weather pattern was the result of a secret agreement reached far above the earth—high, high in the sky—many years before. On that day, the sun, clouds, moon, and stars all agreed to take equal turns on the Sunnyville Weather Stage to display their talents—an arrangement that came to be known as "The Sunnyville Weather Agreement."

In keeping with the terms of the agreement, the sun shone brightly on its special days—Saturday, Sunday, and Monday—to provide light and heat so people could see and keep warm—and also to help the crops, grass, and flowers grow.

Likewise, on Tuesdays and Wednesdays, the clouds showed off their puffy, white coats to provide shade from the sun. Each Thursday, the clouds displayed their versatility by turning dark and shadowy. And on Fridays, they presented the grand finale, opening up their tear ducts and crying from day until night—not because they were sad, mind you, but just to give Sunnyville's people water, and to keep everything green growing.

The sun and clouds performed by turns each day, and the moon shone brilliantly every evening, providing light for the town's nightly dances, carriage rides, hoedowns, and other activities.

Not to be outdone, the stars provided a beautiful backdrop of twinkling lights in the night sky, along with heavenly puzzle shapes called constellations. Some of the most popular shapes had names like

The Big Dipper, The Little Dipper, Pegasus, and The Ram—but there were countless other patterns waiting to be discovered and made famous on the stage of the Sunnyville sky.

Meanwhile, far below in Sunnyville, people spent hours gazing at the stars at night, and challenging each other to see who could find the most shapes, and who could find new ones.

QUIRKY KIND OF GUY

It's worth repeating that when it came to the weather, everyone in Sunnyville was happy—everyone, that is, except Big Bob. Day after day, year after year, he made the same forecasts—saying the same thing, in the same way—according to whatever was scheduled to happen the next day. And, frankly, he was getting pretty tired of the whole routine.

Maybe if he had been an ordinary kind of weatherman, he could have coped with the monotony. The truth was, however, Big Bob was about as far from "ordinary" as a weatherman could possibly be.

You see, even if the weather *hadn't* been the same all the time, Bob had a special way of knowing exactly what kind of weather was coming each day! As strange as it seems, Big Bob had a variety of bodily quirks that pointed to different kinds of weather. Every night, before bed, or shortly before he began his weather forecast, one of the quirks would show up.

On nights before sunny days, for example, his hair would stand up, and his face would turn a bright red. Before partly cloudy days, his hair would suddenly straighten out and part in the middle and his face took on a slightly dark shadow, as if he needed a shave. When rain was on the way, Bob would come down with such a bad case of the giggles, that tears would form in his eyes. Indeed, he had a different quirk for every kind of weather imaginable!

THE PRICE OF BEING DIFFERENT

Bob often wondered why he was burdened with these strange "tics," which first appeared years earlier. From the standpoint of giving his weather reports, he didn't really *need* the quirks, since the weather patterns simply repeated themselves over and over, like clockwork.

Not to mention that his "peculiarities" were embarrassing, and only added to the teasing and bullying he had to put up with at school. The meanest bully in school, Mickey Blowhard, gave him the humiliating nickname, "Freakshow," and it stuck to him like glue—kept alive by other kids, who, unfortunately, followed Mickey's lead.

As often as he could, Mickey would ridicule Bob because of his quirks, punch him when the teachers weren't looking, and post cruel comments about him online.

Along with Bob, Ollie was a target for Mickey's online taunts, as well, because of the attention she and Bob received for their academic achievements.

The two managed to weather it all, however, continuing to do well throughout school, blossoming in their careers, and currently sharing the distinction of being among the most highly regarded young people in all of Sunnyville.

BOB MAKES A WISH

One gloomy Thursday afternoon, Bob sat at his desk, mulling over the countless weather forecasts he had done in the past, plus the ones he was expected to do in the future and he decided he'd had enough. No sooner had he made this decision than he heard a light tap on his door.

"Bob, are you there? It's Ollie." Her familiar, clear voice was laced with concern.

"Come in," Bob said glumly, mirroring both his mood and the dreary weather outside.

Ollie walked in and closed the door behind her. "Bob, you seem sad. What's wrong?" she asked.

"I'm tired of telling people about the same weather all the time!" he cried. "It's *boring* repeating the same things over and over and over again: '*It's going to be another bea-uuu-tiful day!*'" he said, mocking himself. "Why can't we mix it up... have a few surprises? I bet that would keep it interesting."

Ollie stood quietly and listened, not knowing what to say. Finally, she walked over to where Bob sat and gave him a hug. Frustrated and sad, he allowed his head to rest dejectedly against one of her encircling arms.

He could not have known that far above the earth—high, high in the Sunnyville sky—things seemed to be lining up to give him his wish.

CELESTIAL SCHOOL DAYS

Like the people of Sunnyville, the sun, moon, cloud, and star families, were happy with the consistent weather routine each week. The predictable schedule allowed their children to have regular practice so that one day, when the time came, they would be ready to take center stage.

The sun children practiced shining on their special days, as did the moon children. The star children practiced twinkling and making shapes and the cloud children practiced being puffy, chasing colorful sun rays, and making rain.

Each of these children, representing their respective celestial families, attended Cloud Land Celestial Academy all week, in hopes of being chosen to display their skills on the Sunnyville Weather Stage.

They were tested in each of their various classes to track their progress and given report cards at the end of each grading period. There was stiff competition among the celestial children—with the exception, that is, of one child from the cloud family: Arthur "Puf Puf" Cloud.

Puf Puf, as he was fondly called by most, was very popular among all the kids in his class—for that matter, among all the kids at the entire school. He was known both for his happy disposition and his ability to make the other kids laugh. In fact, he spent most of his time, both in and out of school, daydreaming and coming up with new ways to entertain his schoolmates.

Unfortunately, the very things that made Puf Puf popular among his peers, caused him major problems with his parents at home and his teachers in school.

CHALLENGING CHORE

"Puf Puf, your room is an utter disaster!" his mom, Mrs. Angel "Puf" Cloud, would often say. "You need to clean it up *right now!*" she scolded.

Puf Puf's dad, Walter "Windy" Cloud, III, would raise an eyebrow and stare pointedly in Puf Puf's direction. Puf Puf knew that this was his father's silent way of saying, "Do what your mother says, and hurry up about it."

Each time this happened, Puf Puf would go to his room and start to clean in earnest, determined to finish the job and make his parents proud. But, all too soon, he would become distracted by a game—or his music—or thoughts of new ways to make his friends laugh. After a while, he would simply forget why he was there.

Hours later, his mother would come to inspect his room, only to find Puf Puf sorting through his ice crystal collection or playing Snowflake Solitaire—and the room still a mess.

"Puf Puf, you have been in here for *hours,* and this room still looks the same," Mrs. Cloud would say gently, but firmly.

At that moment, Mr. Cloud would appear at Puf Puf's door. "Why, you haven't accomplished a *thing!*" he would sternly observe. "If this room doesn't get *completely* cleaned up in fifteen minutes, there will be *no* playtime for you, Arthur Puf Puf Cloud!"

His dad always used his full name when he was angry.

Usually, when things reached this point, there would be further scolding from Mr. Cloud, followed by tears from Puf Puf, after which he would finally manage, with great difficulty, to rein in his attention long enough to finish the room-cleaning.

PAPERS AND PALS

In school, things followed much the same pattern. When his teachers called upon Puf Puf to participate in class, he was often so busy daydreaming about faraway adventures or thinking of new ways to amuse his friends, that he wasn't paying attention to what the class was doing.

"Arthur?" the teacher would call out. "Can you tell the class when Columbus Cloudy discovered Cloud Land?"

Puf Puf's desk was so disorganized that he usually couldn't find the material for the work they were talking about. *Or*, by the time he *found* what he was looking for, the teacher and class had often moved on to the next subject.

"Uhh, Columbus Cloudy, ma'am?" Puf Puf nervously responded, as he sifted through piles of old and new papers. "Does he have anything to do with math?" he offered hopefully. "Because I've got that homework right here!"

The teacher would drop her head in frustration, and the class would roar with laughter.

"Okay, just give me a minute," Puf Puf would say, still rifling through his papers. When he knew there was no hope, he would finish by asking, "Can you give me a hint?" Again, the class would explode with laughter.

The other kids thought this familiar routine was all part of Puf Puf's act to make them laugh. They got a big kick out of his fumbling through the stacks of jumbled papers. Puf Puf played along as if he had indeed, planned the whole thing, but he was secretly embarrassed that he couldn't keep up.

REPORT CARD DAY

On report card day, the children were excited to receive their grades. Good grades meant the possibility of getting a chance to fill in for their parents on the Sunnyville Weather Stage to get more experience. It also meant rewards from their parents for their efforts in school.

But for Puf Puf, Report Card Day was a time of extreme stress that caused his stomach to ache. His grades at the end of the last grading period were relatively good. He managed an A in Tear Duct Management, a B in Puffiness, and a C in Cloud History. His only bad grades that time were in Organization and Class Participation. In both of those classes, he'd received D's.

This time, he knew that his report card would not be as good. This was especially true of his grades in Cloud Fluffiness and Overcasting—his parents' specialties. He knew for sure that he'd gotten F's in both.

First thing Monday morning, the teacher passed out the report cards to all the students in the class. She congratulated the top students on their efforts and tried to offer consoling words to the students who didn't do as well. When she reached Puf Puf, she shook her head and whispered, "Good luck with your parents. I think you'll need it."

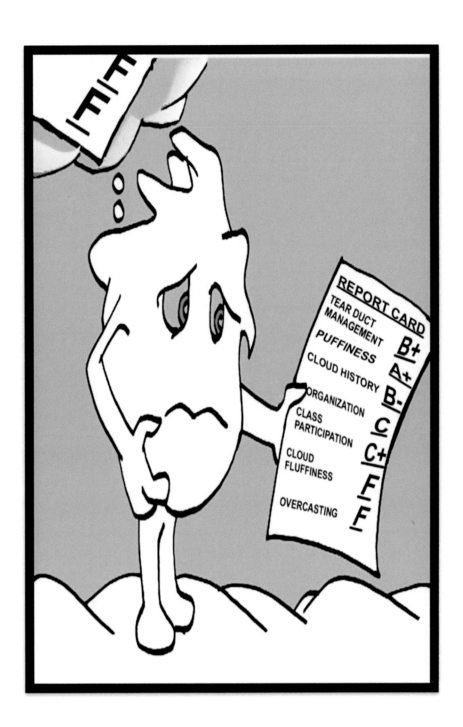

That evening, Mr. and Mrs. Cloud looked over Puf Puf's Report Card, shaking their heads in astonishment. Mr. Cloud turned his gaze toward Puf Puf, who sat slouched in his seat at the table.

Clearing his throat, Mr. Cloud began, "Uh-hmm. What do you have to say for yourself, son?" Despite his frustration over Puf Puf's consistently poor grades, he made an effort to speak in an understanding tone, while Mrs. Cloud looked on sympathetically.

Puf Puf began slowly, "Well, I-I'm sorry I let you down. Mom—I know you're great at fluffiness—and Dad, everyone says you're the best at overcasting. I'm trying my best—but I'm just not good at *any* of it," he said, his face falling.

"I understand that it makes you sad that I'm not," he went on, sounding more and more miserable. "But, I just wish you could find something in the way I am that would make you prouder of me. Then, maybe the things I'm not good at wouldn't make you so unhappy with me," Puf Puf said sadly, getting up from the table and walking towards his room, large tears beginning to roll down his rounded cheeks.

Mr. and Mrs. Cloud looked at each other silently, their own eyes welling with tears.

When Puf Puf reached his room, he cried and cried, more than he had ever cried before. His tears were so plentiful that, far below in Sunnyville, they began to fall in the form of heavy rain.

MONDAY MORNING BLAHS

Big Bob sat in his office at the TV station trying to rev up his spirits so that he could deliver his usual Monday weather forecast.

"Knock-knock," Steve said, punctuating his words with two crisp taps on Bob's office door and continuing down the hallway, never breaking his stride. "Five minutes to air, Bob," he said, his voice floating back from a spot surprisingly far away from where he had just tapped the door seconds ago.

Somewhat amused, Bob snapped his head in the direction Steve's voice had come from, and wondered: *How does that guy manage to get around so quickly?*

Big Bob shook his head slightly, forcing his thoughts back to the task at hand. It was almost airtime, and he needed to begin his warm-up *now!*

A WISH COME TRUE

Bob launched into his usual spiel: "It's another *bea-uuu-tiful....*" All of a sudden, in the middle of his sentence, he began to giggle hysterically.

"Hee-hee-hee-hee-hee! Hah-hah-hah-hah-hah!" Wave after wave of goofy giggles tumbled out of Bob's mouth. In fact, he giggled so much that his eyes began to water. Stunned by the sudden appearance of his rainy-day quirk, he gazed out of his office window.

"A storm!" he cried out in utter astonishment. "Wait a minute—it *can't* be! This is Monday. It's always *sunny* on Mondays! It-it's not possible!" Bob stammered.

He pinched his right arm. "Ouch!" he yelped. "Well, that proves I'm awake," he said, still puzzled. He took a careful look at the calendar. "It's Monday, alright," he assured himself.

Tickled by the mysterious change in the weather pattern, Bob started to laugh uncontrollably. He burst through his office door and began to zip haphazardly from one section of the TV station to another shouting, "It's not possible! It's not possible! It just can't *be*!!" He then proceeded to bolt down the hallway.

"Bob, where on earth are you going—and what's all the shouting about?" Steve demanded. "We have less than a minute to air!" he said, frowning and checking his watch.

WILD, WILD WEATHERMAN!

Ignoring Steve's announcement, Bob continued his mad dash in the opposite direction from where he belonged.

"Bob!!!" Steve called after him frantically.

"10, 9, 8 seconds to air!" said Mike, the news producer.

"Has Bob lost his mind?" Steve asked, bewildered. "Well, don't just stand there!" he yelled to Nick, the cameraman. "Follow him!"

Springing into action, Nick raced outside after Big Bob.

"7, 6, 5..." Mike continued, his voice rising anxiously.

Finally catching up with Big Bob, Nick yelled, "For heaven's sake, man, pull yourself together! We're about to go live on the air!"

But Bob paid no attention whatsoever to the urgent warning and was now laughing and dancing excitedly in large puddles of rain.

"4, 3, 2, 1—you're on the air!" Mike finished, silently mouthing the number "1" along with his final words, and wringing his hands apprehensively, while beads of nervous sweat popped out all over his forehead.

All at once, Big Bob transitioned perfectly to his on-camera personality. "Good evening, folks!" he said to his viewing audience, right on cue. "It's going to be another *bea-uuu-tiful* day in Sunnyville!" He paused, grinning from ear to ear. "And guess what? It's raining!!" Big Bob shouted, as he once again began to laugh and dance in the pouring rain.

23

STATION STATIC

Within minutes, the townspeople of Sunnyville began to file out into the streets in front of their homes in confusion and disbelief. It's not that they had never seen rain. It's just that they had never seen rain on a *Monday*. Questions and complaints began to flood the TV station.

Mrs. Johnson, who always did her laundry on Mondays, wanted to know when she could hang her wash out to dry. Mr. Flannery complained that he had to cancel his regular Monday golf game at the club.

There were so many calls to the station that the customer service reps couldn't handle them all—which, of course, only made a bad situation even worse.

Everyone, it seemed, wanted to talk to Big Bob.

When Bob tried to explain why the weather was the way it was, or how long it was going to be that way, he realized that he couldn't—not because he didn't *want* to—but because he didn't *know!*

None of his training as a weatherman—or any of Sunnyville's weather reference books or historical weather records—could explain what was happening.

THE BLAME GAME

Almost overnight, Big Bob went from being the most popular man in Sunnyville to being the most *un*popular. Someone even came up with a new nickname for him, and it caught on quickly. People were now calling the station and asking to speak to "the rain man"!

Just what I need, thought Bob when he heard about it. *Another sarcastic nickname!*

So many angry letters began to pour in for him that the postman had to get help delivering them. And, after the second day of rain, Bob had to disguise himself just to go to and from work because of all the mean looks and comments from the irate citizens of Sunnyville.

There was no denying that, for Big Bob, the joy of finally getting a break from the usual, boring weather pattern, was dampened by the fact that just about everyone in Sunnyville was angry with him, holding him *personally* responsible for their weather woes.

But what stung Bob even *more*, was realizing that the folks who were angrily waiting to confront him on the street—the folks saying such harsh things about him (even demanding that he be fired unless the rain stopped soon)—these were the very same folks who, just days before, had been among his biggest fans.

BE CAREFUL WHAT YOU WISH FOR....

It was the third day of rain in Sunnyville with no end in sight. Tempers were growing shorter and shorter, and nerves were fraying drop-by-relentless-raindrop.

"Bob, can you come in here?" said Steve as Bob walked past his office door. Steve had deliberately left his door slightly ajar, knowing that Bob would be passing by sooner or later.

Bob noticed immediately the unusually somber note in his boss's voice, and, under the circumstances, it made him distinctly uneasy.

"Sure Steve," Bob said, smiling nervously. He eased the door shut as he entered. "This sure is some strange weather, huh?"

Ignoring Bob's question, Steve shuffled some papers on his desk with his head lowered, as if deep in thought.

"Here's the thing, Bob," Steve said in a reluctant and distracted manner. "We're getting a lot of angry calls and letters, so—either fix this thing or you're out," he finished bluntly, never raising his head from the papers on his desk to look Bob in the eye. "Close the door on your way out," Steve added, before Bob could reply.

A FRIEND INDEED

Dazed, Bob exited his boss's office, closing the door behind him as Steve had instructed. As he walked slowly toward his own office, clusters of staring, whispering coworkers moved aside to let him pass.

Grateful to escape their curiosity, Bob entered his office, and found Ollie waiting for him. He closed the door and flopped into the chair behind his desk. Feeling misunderstood and brokenhearted, he folded his arms on the desk's flat surface, and laid his head on top of his arms. He found himself sitting that way a *lot* lately. Ollie walked over and gently rubbed his shoulder.

"All I wanted was a little variety—to feel like I was doing something other than saying what everybody already knew. Now look at the mess my dreaming has gotten me into. What am I going to do?" he said miserably.

"It'll be alright Bob. You'll see," Ollie said, in the most soothing tone she could muster.

He could tell that she was trying very hard to sound encouraging. As mixed-up and as miserable as he felt right now, a wave of deep gratitude washed over him for Ollie's kindness. Over the years, he had often taken her friendship for granted, but now, more than ever, he realized how important it was.

"I'll be okay," he said quietly. "Thanks for always being there for me." She nodded, giving him a final pat on the shoulder, and left.

For another minute or two, Bob continued to sit, considering the irony of his situation. Just days earlier, a heavy rain had washed away the usual Monday morning monotony, leaving Bob feeling energized and refreshed. Now, that same downpour was threatening to disrupt his life and future, causing uncertainty to swirl around him like a rising storm.

CURIOUS COWORKERS

Bob stood up and prepared to leave. There was nothing to be gained by hanging around the station any longer today. The weather segments on the daily broadcast schedule had been temporarily suspended since no one needed him to tell them what they already knew: IT WAS RAINING!!!

He considered putting some papers in his briefcase to work on at home, as he typically would have, but quickly dismissed the idea and instead, put his briefcase into one of his large desk drawers.

There's no way that I'm going to get any work done tonight, he said to himself.

Empty-handed, he walked to the door. It felt strange to be without his briefcase but then, this whole day had been strange from the very outset.

Opening his office door, he heard whispers and the hurried rustling of feet moving away down the hall. The same staffers and on-air personnel that lined the hallway a few minutes earlier when he'd left Steve's office, had crept closer to his door. Again, they pretended to be having casual conversations, when they were obviously listening for any hint of what might happen next.

Bob ignored them and headed toward the building's main exit. Seconds later, Steve poked his head out of his office door. He stared at the crowd in the hallway, spotting Bob a short distance beyond where the crowd was standing, making his way toward the exit. Pausing just long enough to allow Bob to get few paces farther away, Steve said in a quiet, but firm voice: "Doesn't anybody have a job to do around this place?" The crowd scattered as Steve disappeared back into his office.

FLASHBACK

Once inside, Steve leaned his back heavily against his closed office door, still gripping the inner doorknob with one hand behind his back. He sighed and turned his face, etched with regret, up toward the ceiling. He couldn't believe that it had come to this, but he'd had no choice. Despite his adamant protests, Mr. Kurchaw, the station's owner, had laid down the law.

"If the rain doesn't stop, Bob Fox has to go," he'd insisted.

Steve felt terrible. He had personally hired Bob right out of meteorology school. He chuckled at the thought of Bob's audition tape and his nervous but kooky delivery of the weather report.

Before Bob came on board, Steve was the station's weatherman. He'd found himself doing double and triple duty, eventually taking over the job of News Director and, finally, Station Manager.

As soon as he'd watched the opening seconds of Bob's tape, he started to laugh. Bob had constructed a simulated newsroom out of cardboard—complete with life-sized news anchor figures. He even rigged up a makeshift weather map with construction paper cutouts of clouds and wind. To top it off, he used one of his mother's round, stainless steel mixing bowls as the sun.

It all seemed to be staged in his parents' kitchen. Bob's dad was the cameraman, and the tape featured occasional inadvertent appearances by Bob's mother, as she tried to avoid the camera while preparing dinner behind the cardboard.

COOL UNDER FIRE

A little more than halfway through the tape, a small fire started when Bob pressed too hard as he tried to attach his wind and rain cutouts to the weather map, causing the bottom of the cardboard to drift too close to the stove. Bob's mother screamed, grabbing the fire extinguisher, as she leapt to the rescue.

Meanwhile, Bob never lost his place in his fantasy weathercast, describing the fire as "burning southern heat," and the gust of air from the extinguisher as "a mighty cold blast from the north." From that moment on, Steve knew Bob had the makings of a great weatherman—or maybe an even better comedian!

When Steve told Bob he had the job, Bob was so excited that he forgot to ask about the salary. Whenever he told the story later, Steve always added, "If I had played it right, I think I could have gotten him to pay *me.*"

He had mentored Bob, becoming a proud second dad, and watching him grow into the star that he became in Sunnyville. Steve and his wife, Cathy, had eaten so many dinners at Bob's parents' home—where Bob also lived—that they felt like members of Bob's family.

A SHARED SORROW

A forceful knock on his door made Steve jump, and brought him sharply back to the present. He released his grip on the doorknob, taking a few steps forward toward his desk to make room for his visitor to enter.

"Come in," he said, turning to face the door, standing a foot or so in front of his desk.

One look at Ollie's face as she entered told him she was angry and disappointed. He dropped his head and closed his eyes, bracing himself for her protest.

"Steve, you can't fire Bob! It doesn't make any sense!" she said passionately.

"Ollie, there is nothing that I can do," Steve said sorrowfully. "You *know* I love Bob, but the decision is out of my hands."

Ollie lowered her head and began to cry.

Steve moved immediately to where she stood to comfort her, as tears rolled down his own cheeks.

THE LONG WAY HOME...

Once outside the studio, Bob trudged listlessly about in the pouring rain, wandering aimlessly for perhaps a mile and a half or so before turning his steps toward his home on Melville Street where he lived with his parents.

Few others were moving about in such miserable weather, so no one questioned or approached him, for which he was very grateful. By the time he reached his home at 2357 Melville, he was soaked down to his socks.

His door keys were in one of his pants pockets, but he had neither the strength nor the will to search for them at this point, so he simply leaned one drenched arm against the doorbell, shifting his weight back and forth just enough to cause the bell to ring repeatedly.

Bob's mother hurried to the door, wondering who would be so rude as to ring the doorbell over and over without giving anyone time to answer it. Annoyed, she flung open the door and was stunned to see her son standing there staring blankly as if in a daze, and soaked through from head to toe.

TEAMWORK AND TLC

"My goodness!! Robert Michael Fox, what *are* you thinking? You'll catch your *death!!*' she exclaimed, frantically pulling him through the door and into the house.

"Herbert!! Come quickly!!" shouted Mrs. Fox to her husband. "And bring dry towels and clothes!"

Dr. Abigail Fox was a petite woman, about five feet tall with light brown skin and slightly graying, auburn hair. She looked considerably more youthful than one might expect for a woman of 44.

A practicing psychiatrist, highly esteemed by colleagues and patients alike, Abigail was soft-spoken, with a kind, slender face, and eyes that exuded understanding and warmth. She laughed easily and often—and was known for her compassion towards even the smallest creatures.

"What's all the shouting about Abby?" Dr. Herbert Fox called out as he reached the front of the house, almost out of breath from running.

"Bobby!!" Dr. Fox cried out in shock. "What in the blazes...?" he trailed off as he looked at his son, who was now being dried with paper towels that Mrs. Fox had hastily retrieved from the kitchen.

"Don't just stand there Herbert! Get me some dry towels, and help me get him to the bathroom," Abigail said with urgency.

Dr. Herbert Fox was a surgeon, who, like his wife, was 44 years old, and had graduated at the top of his medical school class, as had she.

He was brown-skinned, with a long, slender face, and dark, brown eyes, and wore his hair cut short to conceal the gray. Well-built and tall at 6-foot-2, he was considered handsome, by most standards of measure.

Herbert and Abigail each took one of Bob's arms and guided him gently to the guest bathroom. Herbert then hurried to the linen closet to grab a large stack of towels, stopping by the laundry room on the way back to gather dry clothes. He and Abigail rubbed vigorously over every inch of their son's soaking wet 6-foot-4 frame, and then insisted that he change into the dry clothing.

PARENTAL POWWOW

By the time Bob emerged from the bathroom, Abigail had placed a steaming hot bowl of her famous chicken soup, left over from earlier in the week, on the table for him, along with a cup of hot lemon tea.

Herbert made her laugh as she warmed up the food, playfully calling it "chicken soup for the soaked!" referencing the well-known inspirational book series. Their shared laughter served to lighten the mood a bit and help them put the dramatic events of the last hour or so into perspective.

Now, she and Herbert sat and waited patiently while Bob slowly ate the soup and sipped his tea. Occasionally, they glanced at each other with concern, understanding all too well the cause of their son's current state. Neither said a word, however.

This was not the first crisis Bob had faced in his life. He had grappled with being "different" when his quirks began to appear. He had been the target of cruelty and bullying in school. And there had been other challenges....

Sometimes, entirely by his own choice, Bob would pour out his heart to his parents and they would listen, empathize, and offer encouragement. These times of heartfelt sharing seemed to help him move forward and they were glad to offer their support.

If it was time, once again, for such a talk, Herbert and Abigail knew from past experience that Bob would have to be allowed to begin the conversation. In the meantime, they were content to remain silent, knowing that their son would open up—if and when he was ready to do so.

SHOWDOWN IN CLOUD LAND

High up above, in Cloud Land, the celestial community was in just as much of an uproar over the unwanted weather changes as the people of Sunnyville were. It was the third day by now, and they were all upset that Puf Puf's crying and the resulting rain, was disrupting the regular schedule.

Late that afternoon, a large, angry crowd gathered in front of Puf Puf's house. Every family in the collective sky community was represented. Mr. Sunny Ray Sun was chosen to be the spokesperson.

Twinkie Star—who was well known for his loud and bossy ways— spoke first. "Now Sunny, make sure Walter understands that this isn't personal," Twinkie said, coaching his neighbor. "Walter and his family are nice folks and all but this is just unacceptable—it's messing up the schedule for everybody!" Mr. Star finished in a huff, as the crowd grumbled in agreement.

"Okay, okay, does one of *you* want to do this or do you want *me* to handle it?" Mr. Sun said, looking out over the huge gathering with slight irritation.

Taking a deep breath to steady his nerves, he reluctantly wobbled to the Cloud family's door and rang the doorbell.

At the sound of the bell, Walter Cloud looked at his wife, raising his fluffy eyebrows questioningly. "Are we expecting anybody?" he asked.

Angel Cloud responded with an elongated, "No-o-o," the questioning rise in her voice revealing that she too was surprised.

Mutually curious as to who their visitor might be, Mr. and Mrs. Cloud both went to the door and were shocked to see all their relatives, friends

and neighbors—in fact, the entire weather and sky community—
gathered on their front lawn.

DESIGNATED SPOKESPERSON

"How can I help you Sunny, and what's all of this about?" Mr. Cloud asked firmly, as he looked out over the crowd.

"Well... uh, Walter...you see, um..." Mr. Sun began haltingly.

"Stop stuttering, Sunny, and speak up! *They* know why we're here!" Mr. Star chimed in, followed by a collective murmur of agreement from the crowd.

"Twinkie, if you don't hush up, you can come up here and do this *yourself.* How'd you like *that?*" Sunny said, challenging Twinkie and all of his neighbors.

"What's this about, Sunny?" Walter Cloud repeated impatiently.

"Well, Walter—it's about Arthur—I mean, uh—Puf Puf," Sunny said, getting started finally.

"Yeah, that's right! *Now,* ya getting to it!" shouted Mr. Star.

"Hush, Twinkie!" chided Mrs. Star, as both Walter and Sunny glanced sternly in his direction.

"You see, Walter—we understand that Puf Puf is having his problems in school—and God knows, it's not easy for us parents to figure out how to deal with our kids' challenges. I mean—we all sympathize with you and Angel," he continued, turning briefly to the crowd for support.

A smattering of affirming sounds came from random sections of the crowd.

"We've all got kids that—well, you know—that don't quite make the grade." He paused, gathering his courage. "But, you *have* to do something about Puf Puf's crying—it has *got* to stop! It's messing things up for *everyone!*" Sunny ended in a rush, grateful to have finished his speech.

"Yeah!!" said Twinkie Star. "You should have *started* with that, Sunny, instead of mealy-mouthing along," he said. Rolling his eyes with annoyance, he added, "We all could've been home by now!"

The murmurs from the crowd seemed to say that they all agreed.

Mrs. Star glanced toward her husband, shaking her head in embarrassment as she looked at Sunny, Walter, and Angel apologetically.

A HEAVENLY SOLUTION

As he continued to cry, Puf Puf heard the commotion outside, and moved from his room to get closer to the front door to hear what was going on. There seemed to be a *big* crowd in their yard. His parents were standing in the open doorway facing the gathering outside, so he eased quietly to a spot behind the door. From there, he would be able to hear all that was being said.

Unaware of Puf Puf's presence, Mr. Cloud looked angrily at Sunny and then at the crowd. His white fluffiness changed to a deeper shade of gray.

"Calm down, Walter, no need to get upset," said Mrs. Cloud soothingly as she stroked his back.

"Yeah Walt, I mean—we've been friends for a long time. I didn't mean to offend you and Angel," said Sunny, with genuine concern.

Mr. Cloud took a deep breath and smiled tenderly at his wife as he patted her hand. He turned to Sunny Sun, his color now fading to a lighter shade of gray as he calmed himself.

Looking thoughtfully over the crowd, he started to speak. "Let me begin by saying, I apologize to you all for the inconvenience we have caused you," he offered sincerely. "But, let me be clear," he continued. "We have never been prouder of Arthur than we are today," Mr. Cloud stated, his voice trembling a bit with emotion.

Caught off guard by his unexpected words, the crowd began to mutter in confusion.

Then Twinkie Star said loudly, "I always knew Walter was cuckoo."

Mr. Cloud ignored Twinkie's outburst and continued. "Several days ago, Arthur taught my wife and me a lesson that I believe is important to us all. You see, we learned that our priorities in the sky community are in the wrong place. We value this *process*—this *schedule*—more than we value our *children*! If our kids aren't perfect or—in *your* words, Sunny—if they 'don't quite make the grade,' there is no place for them."

Mr. Cloud took a moment to choose his next words carefully, wanting everyone present to follow his reasoning. "The schedule ought to celebrate what our children *can* do, not highlight what they *can't*. We ought to be more proud of their *talents*, than embarrassed about their *challenges*," he said. He paused and was encouraged to see that they all still seemed to be listening intently. In fact, it was quiet enough to hear a snowflake fall.

THIS LITTLE LIGHT OF HIS

Looking now at Twinkie, Mr. Cloud said, "Twinkie, you are the greatest twinkler and puzzle-maker that I've ever seen—heck, who knows, maybe the best *ever*!"

At this, Twinkie Star began to swell with pride.

"And you've trained your children well to follow in your footsteps," Mr. Cloud continued.

"You got *that* right!" Twinkie agreed, with a nod of his radiant head.

"But what about your son, Shooter?" Mr. Cloud asked evenly. "He just can't seem to hold his place in the patterns. He just shoots off and does his own thing," he said, looking steadily at his neighbor.

"Now, you wait just a minute, Walter—" Twinkie Star began angrily.

"Calm down, Twinkie," Walter Cloud said calmly. "I'm only saying this to make my point."

Focusing his attention on the crowd, he asked, "Isn't it time for us to celebrate the things that don't fit into the schedule?"

Turning back to Twinkie, Mr. Cloud said kindly, "I've noticed that when Shooter does his own thing, he leaves a beautiful trail of colors. Why can't there be a special place for *that* in the schedule? And why not *recognize* Shooter for his uniqueness?"

Touched by Mr. Cloud's expression of appreciation for his son, Twinkie Star looked tearfully at his wife and nodded his head in agreement. "I always thought the boy was talented.... Maybe that Walter is not so crazy, after all," he admitted, somewhat grudgingly.

SOMETHING'S HAPPENING!

From his safe spot behind the door, Puf Puf had been listening carefully to his father's words. He had never heard his dad talk this way before. He certainly hadn't expected to hear, after the awful report card he'd brought home, that his parents were *proud* of him, or that *they* had learned something from *him*. But, he was able to understand most of what his father had said and it all made him feel good inside—better than he had felt since Report Card Day on Monday. He didn't quite know how to explain it, but it felt to him as if something important was happening—or maybe was *about* to happen—and he didn't want to miss *any* of it.

A CHANCE TO SHINE

Walter Cloud now scanned the crowd, searching for a particular face. "Moonie?" he called out, soon finding his neighbor.

Directing his attention to Mr. and Mrs. Moonie Moon, he said, "You and the Mrs. have great kids that are chips off the old block." Walter hesitated briefly. "But what about Crescent and Quarter?" he asked, deliberately stating the question as gently as possible.

"Yeah!" Twinkie Star butted in. "If you put those two together, they *still* wouldn't be able to make a full moon," he chuckled.

"Twinkie!!" Mrs. Star said sharply, still trying in vain to shush her husband.

"I'm just saying," Mr. Star finished, with an unapologetic shrug of his shoulders.

"Uh-hmm," said Walter Cloud, clearing his throat. "My point," he said, staring impatiently in Mr. Star's direction before turning back to the Moon family, "is that those are shapes that don't get nearly as much recognition and positive feedback as the full moon does."

A low buzz went through the crowd as everyone acknowledged that this was, indeed, the case.

"Maybe it's time to let Crescent and Quarter—plus all the in-between shapes in your family—know that they're valuable and important, too, and just as deserving of their place in the schedule as the larger, more prominent shapes," said Mr. Cloud.

In a final appeal to Moonie and his family, which Mr. Cloud hoped all the others present would take to heart in their own families, he said: "Shouldn't all the members of the moon family have an opportunity to be themselves and do what they do best? And shouldn't you and the Mrs. be proud of them, too, when it's their turn to shine?"

The crowd fell silent for a moment as they considered Mr. Cloud's words, and then the entire gathering burst spontaneously into enthusiastic applause.

Mr. and Mrs. Cloud embraced each other as Mrs. Cloud whispered softly, "I'm proud of you, Walter."

As Mr. Cloud held his wife, he noticed Puf Puf standing behind the door. He nodded to his son affectionately, secretly winking his eye. Puf Puf's face held the beginnings of a smile as—for the first time in days—the flow of his tears slowed to a stop.

MAKING CHANGES

Later that day, committees were formed throughout the sky community, led by Walter Cloud. After talking things through, the groups decided that schools would not only focus on and grade basic subjects, like reading and history, but they would also seek to identify and encourage each child's individual talents. At last, Puf Puf, and other students like him, would no longer be made to feel less valuable than their fellow classmates.

Likewise, the weekly weather schedule was changed to allow each and every child to display his or her gifts.

Puf Puf, for example, was now truly appreciated for his happy disposition and for always being on hand to keep the children and their parents laughing.

And he *loved* getting a chance to open up his tear ducts to bring rain when it was his turn, which—as had recently become abundantly clear—he was *very* good at doing!

Puf Puf was now so excited about school that he worked extra hard to keep up without being told and his grades, while not perfect, were mostly A's and B's.

Mr. and Mrs. Cloud and the other parents were extremely proud and happy to see Puf Puf and the other children enjoying school more and feeling so much better about their own special talents and the things they were able to do well.

THE SUNNYVILLE SHUFFLE

Big Bob sat at his office desk in despair, his arms folded on the desk and his head resting on his arms—*again.* He couldn't help but wonder: *Could this really be the end of my career as Sunnyville's weatherman?*

Just then, his hair began to stand up and his face turned bright red. "Yes! *Yes!!*" Big Bob cried out excitedly. "This can only mean one thing—I hope!" He jumped up and ran to his office window, and was delighted to find that, just as his face and hair indicated, the sun was emerging, and the rain had stopped. As suddenly as it had started, it had stopped!!

"I *did* it! I *did* it! I *did* it!" Bob shouted gleefully as he ran down the hall to Steve's office and burst through the door.

"What's all the racket about *now*, Bob?" said Steve, slightly shaken by Bob's dramatic entrance.

"Look out of the window, Steve—I did it! Well, uh, I didn't do it *technically*," he admitted awkwardly. "But, the rain has stopped!"

Before Bob could even finish his sentence, Steve jumped up and ran to his window. "By golly Bob, you did it! You *did* it!" he said, looking back at Bob in wonder. "Well, uh—you didn't really *do* it," he said, pausing briefly, "—but, however it happened, it's just in the nick of time!"

He grabbed Bob and began to dance around his office.

Ollie came running through Steve's office door, not bothering to knock. "Bob, you *did* it!!!" she said excitedly, joining in on the dance.

"There's only one problem," Bob said. "It's Thursday, and according to the schedule, it should be dreary and overcast."

"Never mind that!" Steve said. "At least it's not raining!"

With Bob and Ollie firmly in tow, Steve set the pace and they all giddily danced the conga around the room, while he happily chanted in time with their steps: "*You-get-to-keep-your-job—oh! I-get-to-keep-my-job—oh! You-get-to-keep-your-job—oh! I-get-to-keep-my-job—oh! You-get-to…!*"

WEATHER WHIZ KID!

In the days that followed, Sunnyville's weather was almost never the same from day to day. As the townspeople slowly began to adapt, the weather and its changes became the most popular topic of conversation in town. People were excited to see what each day would bring.

They had now seen days that were windy, icy and snowy, plus all kinds of strange and unexpected combinations—and they loved it!

The only constant was Big Bob's mind-boggling wizardry in predicting the next day's weather. Each night before—or sometimes even *during*—the weathercast, his strange, yet familiar, bodily quirks would show up, making Bob's weather report the highest rated show in town.

Everyone began to think of Big Bob as a bona fide weather wizard. People watched eagerly to see if the quirks would come out during the show. When they did, it was always exciting and good for a laugh.

Bob played it up to make it fun for both himself and his audience. He would put his hand on his back when it throbbed and do the bunny-hop to predict snow. To predict a windy day, he would grab his knee when it hurt and begin break dancing.

Once again, Bob was the most popular man in town and the happiest he had ever been.

One day, just before he was about to go on the air, Big Bob thought back to the time when he'd had to pretend to be happy while giving the daily weather report. Now, as he faced his television audience, his smile was sincere and came straight from his heart.

"5, 4, 3, 2, 1—" said Mike, the producer, silently mouthing the "1" and pointing his forefinger at Bob with a dramatic flourish.

It was *showtime!!* And the weather wizard was ready!

"And tonight's weather, folks—" Big Bob said in a booming voice, pausing to let the suspense build, while allowing his quirk to come out fully. "Wait a minute—I feel it coming...." he said, as one side of his hair straightened out and he got a small case of the giggles. This time, it was only enough to produce a wisp of a tear.

Taking a breath, he smiled and said brightly: "Cloudy—with a chance of rain!"

◊◊◊◊◊

Made in the USA
Lexington, KY
17 August 2019

Cloudy with a Chance of Rain, is a magical tale that celebrates the need for understanding and inclusion while touching upon the current challenges many of our children face and their journey to overcome. The book explores the power of a heartfelt wish to shake-up the die-cast routines and traditions of a community, while setting in motion powerful ripples of creative change and transformation.

The story's action focuses on two very different communities—the quaint and comfortable little town of Sunnyville, while the other is located high, high in the sky above the earth in a magical place called Cloud Land. The collision between the two sets off a domino-like adventure propelled by an age-old secret, a funny and popular weatherman who is actually a weather wizard; a lovable little cloud who, try as he might, cannot manage to fit into the patterns set by his parents; and a surprise weather snafu that sparks a revolt in both worlds.

www.cloudywithachanceofrain.org

ISBN 9781717400321

90000 >

9 781717 400321

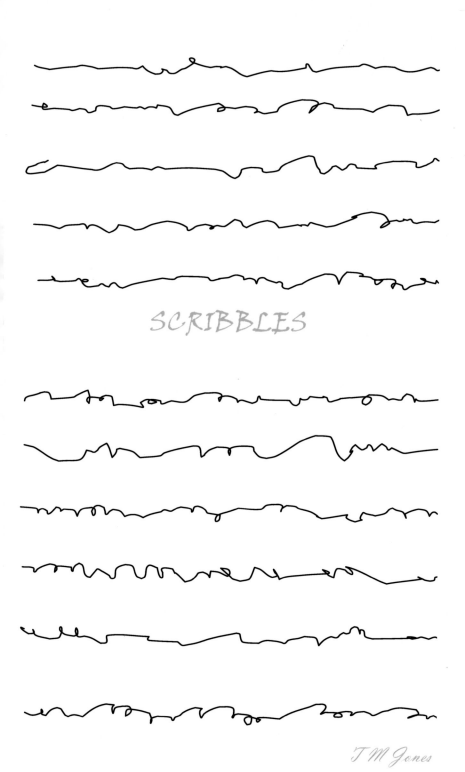

To Kayla
I really appreciate
your support. I wish you
well in all your travels &
future plans. Enjoy. Let me
know if you find something that touches you
Always be happy always be blessed
xoxo Tanya